ote 6

BY J. L. SMITH

The Abominators

The Abominators in the Wild

The Abominators and the Forces of Evil

The ABOMINATORS

IN THE WILD

My PANTY WANTY WOOS Save the day!

J. L. SMITH

ILLUSTRATED BY SAM HEARN

LITTLE, BROWN BOOKS FOR YOUNG READERS
lbkids.co.uk

LITTLE BROWN BOOKS FOR YOUNG READERS

First published in Great Britain in 2012 by Little Brown Books for Young Readers

A CIP catalogue record for this book
is available from the British Library.

ISBN 978-1-907411-63-2

Typeset in Golden Cockerel by M Rules
Printed and bound in Great Britain by
Clays Ltd, St Ives plc

Papers used by LBYR are from well-managed forests
and other responsible sources.

MIX
Paper from
responsible sources
FSC   www.fsc.org   FSC® C104740

Little Brown Books for Young Readers
An imprint of
Little, Brown Book Group
100 Victoria Embankment
London EC4Y 0DY

An Hachette UK Company
www.hachette.co.uk

www.lbkids.co.uk

For the Anderson Boys . . .

Jamie, Ally, Davie, Jack the Cat

and Moustache-Bash

It was a slightly chilly September-ish sort of a morning. Probably because it was September. The kids of Grimely East Primary School gathered in the playground, clutching new lunchboxes and hoping nobody would notice their embarrassing start-of-a-new-school-year haircuts.

Four grubby children lurked suspiciously by the bike sheds. They looked shifty, as if

they had been up to something. In actual fact, they hadn't done anything. Yet. They were the most mischievous gang in the school, the first children the teachers suspected when anything loud, or messy, or disastrous happened. They were the Abominators.

For the first time, the Abominators had been forced to be apart over the summer holidays. Three of them had been sent away, and the other was kept under close supervision. This was because the previous summer they had:

* Ruined Grimely's annual clog dancing festival, by releasing a hundred mice in the town square

* Switched all labels on the jams and preserves at the county show, leading to a spectacular free-for-all handbag fight between the members of the Women's Guild
* Halted production at the Grimely cheese factory for three days, with just one homemade stink bomb

* Caused confusion at the
  local home for the
  elderly, by pretending
  to be visitors and
  eating all the biscuits
* Forced the Mayor to declare
  a State of Emergency, when
  they posted leaflets through
  everybody's door saying that
  Grimely was officially at war with
  Peru.

It had been the best summer, *ever*. Unlike this
summer, which had been boring in comparison.

"So, whad'ya do in the holidays, then?"
asked Mucker, their leader.

"Me and my sister, we were sent to our
granddad's farm," said Cheesy (whose pointy face,
twitchy nose and round, pink ears made him

look more mouse-like than ever). "It was very quiet. Even the *sheep* were quiet. But, one night, I got up and went downstairs to fetch a glass of water. Turns out he's only got a burglar alarm! I've never heard anything so loud! Sirens. Klaxons. The lot. My granddad came rushing out with a shotgun!"

"Bet you were in loads of trouble," said Bob (the only girl in the gang, who was really called Ruby). She grinned, flicking her long pigtail over her shoulder. Without it, Bob could easily pass for a boy. She walked exactly like a boy, she talked exactly like a boy and – despite a wardrobe full of girls' clothes – she dressed exactly like a boy.

"I was in even more trouble when I let the piglets loose in the pen where he keeps his geese." Cheesy grinned. When he was away from his strict parents, Cheesy took every chance he could to follow the Abominators Code of Conduct – to cause trouble and mayhem at every opportunity. "They made the burglar alarm sound *quiet*. Granddad was so angry, he went purple!"

"Nice one," said Mucker, approvingly.

"Dad took me to a holiday camp cos he was singing in a cabaret," said Boogster, playing it cool because he knew the others would be jealous. "One night, I swapped all the keys behind the reception desk. Nobody could get into their chalets!"

"I wish I'd seen that!" said Bob, with a laugh.

"That was nothing. On curry night, I stole all the loo paper!" Boogster grinned at the memory. "How about you, Mucker? How was your holiday?"

"Sent to our Auntie Eileen's," said Mucker,

gloomily. "We played football mostly and camped in her back garden. After the first day she wouldn't have us in her house."

"Why not?" asked Cheesy.

"We broke all her ornaments," said Mucker. "And we got tomato ketchup on her curtains. And we flooded her bathroom, so the kitchen ceiling collapsed. Oh, and we accidentally dyed her cat blue. It looked *awesome*, but she didn't think so."

"Everybody got to have fun except me," moaned Bob. "I was stuck here in Grimely. It was the worst summer ever. Mum made me go shopping, and bake cakes with sugar substitute, and do everything I hate."

The Abominators groaned in sympathy. They all knew how Bob's mother despaired of ever getting her daughter to wear pink and enjoy baking, however much she wanted her to.

"That's well rubbish," said Cheesy, sympathetically.

"Not only that," said Bob, "but I kept bumping into ... oh, watch out – here he comes now!"

A skinny boy of their age, his clean blond hair combed in a centre parting, was running towards them across the playground. His arms were open wide as if he was about to hug them

My FRIENDS! I've missed you so MUCH! At last we're together again!

all, his eyes shone with joy, and he had the biggest grin on his face you could imagine.

As he came closer he started shouting: "MY FRIENDS! I've missed you SO MUCH! At last we're together again! I am AS HAPPY AS A CLAM!"

"Bob," hissed Boogster, "why *did* you tell him he could be an associate member of the gang?"

"I have *no* idea," said Bob, staring at the excited figure approaching them.

*

Cecil Trumpington-Potts was delighted to be going back to Grimely East Primary School after the summer holidays.

He had really missed his new friends.

At the end of last term he had been made an associate member of the Abominators gang – but then the summer holidays had arrived, and he had not seen them for six whole weeks.

They had all been away except Bob, and every time he had seen her, she had been with her mum and had rushed off in the opposite direction saying she had something important to do.

So Cecil had spent a quiet summer with his father, going to the Job Centre (Cecil's father, Lord Trumpington-Potts, was *still* unemployed) and the library, and to Grimely's famous Bucket Museum (famous for its collection of modern and antique buckets from around the world), where they'd ended up volunteering, just for something to do.

Cecil had become quite expert at polishing buckets, while his dad had put his great knowledge of the history of buckets to good use and acted as a guide for visitors.

Cecil's teacher, Miss Jeffries, who also volunteered at the museum, had praised Cecil's dad handsomely. On one occasion, after

Miss Jeffries commented on his bucket-related expertise, Lord Trumpington-Potts had been so pleased and flustered, he had polished the next three buckets with his beard (which was the longest in England) instead of his duster.

"If only I had a *real* job," Lord Trumpington-Potts had said wistfully to Cecil, "then all of our problems would be solved."

Money had been tight since Lord Trumpington-Potts had lost the family fortune and they had had to leave Trumpington Manor. But while his father was finding life in the real world difficult, Cecil had never been happier.

He had been so excited the night before the beginning of term he could hardly sleep. "I can hardly sleep!" Cecil had told his father a hundred times. "Tomorrow, I'm seeing my friends! I'm so happy I could *explode!*"

*

In another part of Grimely, someone else had struggled to go to sleep: the head teacher of Grimely East Primary, Mr Nutter.

"Tomorrow, I've got to go back and be a headmaster again," he had thought to himself, as he lay awake.

"Never mind, dear," his wife Ima had said in her sleep, as if she could read his mind.

Cecil reached the Abominators and – to their relief – instead of hugging them, he just jumped up and down waving his arms.

"I can't BELIEVE it's school again at LAST!" he cried. "I'm *so pleased* to see you that if I was a doggie I'd be wagging my little tail! I'm so excited, I could make a wee-wee!"

Cecil had been brought up by a very old-fashioned nanny called Mabel Drudge, who had only ever spoken to him in baby talk, so he thought that it was perfectly ordinary to talk this way. Despite the gang trying to teach him to talk normally, he still slipped into it without thinking.

"*Chill*, Cecil," said Mucker. He reached up, trying to give Cecil a high five. But Cecil misunderstood and grabbed Mucker's hand,

twirling so they were dancing like two mad ballerinas.

The others laughed as Mucker shook off Cecil indignantly.

"We've got Mr Coleman as our new teacher for Year 6," said Bob. "He's not as soft as Miss Jeffries."

"Certainly not," Cecil agreed. "His skin looks much rougher. I don't think he uses moisturiser."

"Not his *skin*, you idiot." Boogster shook his head. "We mean that he won't let us get away with stuff like she did. He'll give more detentions."

"Oh, goodie!" Cecil jumped up and down, clapping his hands together like a three year old. "I *love* detentions! More time with my friendy-wendies!"

"Please don't call us your friendy-wendies,

Cecil," pleaded Cheesy. "It isn't . . . *normal*. If you're in the gang, you've got to be cool."

"Everyone keeps telling me to chill and to be cool," said Cecil, puzzled, "but I'm already chilling my botty off!" While the rest of the children were in trousers, Cecil was still in his school summer shorts.

"Cecil," said Mucker wearily, "you may have read the complete works of Shakespeare, and you may be able to speak five languages . . . but you've got *a lot* to learn!"

2

Mr Coleman took a deep breath and looked at the class. He'd been feeling uneasy all summer: the thought that he had to teach the Abominators for a whole year had quite spoiled his holidays. Even when he'd been sitting in a deckchair on the beach, enjoying an ice cream, he'd had a terrible feeling of looming disaster.

It was the back row that was the problem. Four dirty, scowling faces and, right beside them, one very clean, smiling face. A face that was positively glowing with enthusiasm. A face that Mr Coleman had been dreading all summer: the face of Cecil Trumpington-Potts.

"Welcome to Year 6!" Mr Coleman said. "This is an important year for you all. You have to grow up and take your lessons seriously. There will be more homework and less messing around in class."

There was a small "boo" from the back row, then Cecil joined in: "BOO! BOOOOOOOOOOOO!"

"Cecil!" Mr Coleman banged on his desk. "I will not tolerate bad behaviour in my classroom. Detention after school!"

"Thank you, sir!" beamed Cecil.

Mr Coleman composed himself.

"However, it's not all doom and gloom. There will also be fun things this year. Such as our camping expedition next month. We'll be camping and trekking in the mountains for three days. It will be a wonderful, character-building experience! And Miss Jeffries will be accompanying us." Mr Coleman stared dreamily into the distance as he said her name.

There was a murmur of excitement around the class. Cecil bounced up and down in his chair. "HOORAY!" he shouted. "I've always wanted to go camping! Tents! Doing a poo in the woods! Singing around the campfire!"

Mr Coleman banged the desk again. "*How many times*, Cecil? No shouting, jumping, squealing or talking in class! If you continue like this, I will have to send you to see Mr Nutter."

"I'm sorry, sir," said Cecil. "I will try not to be a silly-billy. But, sir, can I ask you a question?"

"If you must, Cecil; what is it?"

"If we're camping for three days, how many pairs of panty wanty woos should I take? I'd guess four pairs, but then perhaps I will get muddy and dirty. They fold up very small –shall I take ten pairs . . . or maybe twenty?"

Mr Coleman looked puzzled. "'Panty wanty woos'? What on *earth* are you talking about?"

"He means his pants, sir," said Mucker, with a perfectly straight face. 'That's what he calls them. He wears them to cover up his botty-wotty, don't you, Cecil?"

"I do!" said Cecil, smiling.

The whole class was laughing, as Mr Coleman grew redder and redder.

"So, sir," persisted Cecil, "should I take lots, just to be on the safe side?"

Mr Coleman had had enough. "Take a *hundred* of them if that will make you happy, Cecil, but can we please all settle down!"

At lunchtime, while Mr Coleman lay down in the staffroom with a cool flannel on his forehead, the Abominators enjoyed shepherd's pie for lunch. Cecil ate three helpings.

"How come you're so skinny, seeing as you eat so much?" asked Bob, as Cecil came back to the table with a particularly large helping of rhubarb crumble and custard.

"I have my main meal at lunch," said Cecil, "because we don't have much to eat at home. Father can't cook so we eat mainly baked beans out of tins, and we have a lot of radishes. "

"Don't you have servants to cook you great feasts?" Cheesy was curious. "I thought you were posh."

"Not any more," said Cecil. "My father spent all the Trumpington-Potts fortune and now he can't get a job. Do you know what? I'm the poorest boy in Grimely!"

There was a silence as the Abominators digested this surprising fact, along with their rhubarb crumble.

"You don't seem bothered about it. Don't you mind?" said Mucker.

"No, not at all," said Cecil, stuffing another huge spoonful of crumble into his mouth. "I'm seeing more of my father than before and, better still, I'm seeing the *real world*. I'm having the best time I've had in my life *ever*! The only bad thing is that I miss Nanny Drudgy, and my pet bear, Boris."

"Did you really have a bear?" Boogster was excited by the idea.

"Yes, but Boris had to be sent to Grimelyshire Safari Park when Trumpington Manor was sold. It's all right, though, as I visited him in the holidays and he seems happy. He's met some other bears and lives in a big enclosure. I'll take you to meet him sometime – I'd like him to see I've got new friends."

Cecil went up to get more rhubarb crumble.

"So he's poorer than *we* are!" said Mucker in

wonder. "Would you believe it? Now *that's* a turn-up!"

"I feel sorry for him if all he's got to eat is tinned beans and radishes," said Bob. "His dad must be proper rubbish."

"He must not be used to doing stuff for himself," said Cheesy, "being a lord and all that. He probably had a servant to choose what socks he was going to wear!"

"If Cecil's going to be following us round," said Mucker, "there's one thing that has to change. We've got to get him to get rid of those ridiculous 'panty wanty woos'. It's an embarrassment, especially when we're changing for PE or something. I mean, they're like *girls'* pants, all silk with that stupid crest on them. We'll have to tell him."

"Not now," said Bob, who could see Cecil making his way back to the table, grinning happily to himself. "Let him enjoy his crumble. I'll talk to him before the school trip – you can count on me. I'll make sure he doesn't bring them with him. Trust me. It's sorted."

When Cecil got home from school, he found his father mopping the floor of their tiny bedsit. He was wearing a pink flowery apron and yellow rubber gloves.

"I think I'm getting the hang of this cleaning business," he said seriously. "Swoosh, swoosh, *squeeze*-it-in-the-bucket. Swoosh, swoosh, *squeeze*-it-in-the-bucket. How was school?"

"Fantastically, brilliantly, incredibly

marvellous . . . or, as my new friends would say, AWESOME!" said Cecil. "Two good things happened. First, I got detention again. And second, there's going to be a school trip!" Cecil rummaged in his school rucksack and pulled out a letter with a tear-off slip attached. "You have to fill in this form."

Lord Trumpington-Potts removed his rubber gloves, put on his monocle and read the letter from Mr Nutter.

"This letter says that pupils have to pay fifty pounds towards the cost of the trip, by Friday!" Lord Trumpington-Potts was horrified. "Cecil, my boy, we don't have that sort of money!"

"But, Father, Mr Coleman took me aside and said that pupils whose parents don't have jobs – like you – don't have to pay."

Lord Trumpington-Potts's face clouded over. "The Trumpington-Pottses DO NOT accept charity!" he thundered in indignation. "I am sorry, Cecil, but you *cannot go on the trip!*"

Cecil sat down on the one chair in the bedsit. He was feeling very strange.

"I am feeling very strange, Father," he said. "What do you think is wrong with me?"

Lord Trumpington-Potts patted him on the head.

"I am afraid, Cecil, that, possibly for the first time in your life, you are feeling disappointed. *That* is what your strange feeling is."

But at that moment Cecil let out the most enormous burp his father had ever heard. It was so impressive, the walls of the bedsit shook. It went on and on and on, lasting for at least ten seconds.

"That's better!" Cecil said at last. "It must be all the radishes!" He looked as happy as ever, with not one trace of disappointment about him.

"But what about the trip?" asked Lord Trumpington-Potts, perplexed.

"Oh, I'm going on the trip, Father," said Cecil, confidently. "All I have to do is get fifty pounds by Friday. I think I'd better find my notebook. I've got some planning to do!"

Cecil stayed up late into the night, scribbling in his Grimely Bucket Museum notebook with his Grimely Bucket Museum pencil. He drew some pictures of himself holding piles of money. Then he wrote a list of possible ways to get money, which included the following ideas:

IDEA 1. Getting people to pay to have their photograph taken with the man with the longest beard in England. Problems: a) no camera b) people might not want their photo taken with the man with the longest beard in England.

IDEA 2. Selling individual radishes for £5 each, making a huge profit. Problem: most people don't like radishes enough to pay £5 for them.

IDEA 3. Busking in town centre. Problem: very bad singer and can't play any musical instrument.

IDEA 4. Robbing a bank. Problem: would go to prison.

Even the loud snores of his father rumbling like distant thunder from beneath his enormous beard could not distract Cecil from his task.

After writing down another twenty ideas and finding problems with every single one of them, the twenty-first idea came to him. And there did not seem to be any problems with it. At last he had a plan, and Cecil finally fell asleep with a great big smile on his face.

By the time Lord Trumpington-Potts woke up the next day, Cecil was already gone. For the next few mornings, the boy left very early for school. Then, on Friday morning, he announced to his father that he had the money.

"How *on earth* did you manage that?" asked Lord Trumpington-Potts in wonder.

"I've been at the train station, Father," answered Cecil proudly, "providing an

important service. I've been polishing people's shoes! I've polished over thirty pairs of them!"

"But . . . how did you get the shoe polish and the brushes? We don't have any money!"

"Oh, I didn't use polish and brushes, Father. I used some of your fine linen handkerchiefs and my own spit. It was incredibly effective. I spat on people's shoes and rubbed very hard until the shoes looked shinier."

"And people *paid* you to spit on their shoes?" Lord Trumpington-Potts was astounded.

"Yes, Father," said Cecil, excitedly, "they couldn't wait! As soon as I spat on their shoes they would get out their money and pay me. One man actually paid *before* I spat on his shoes, and he practically *begged* me to not clean them! He gave me five pounds! But I cleaned his shoes anyway. I did an extra huge spit for him because he'd been so generous. He was completely lost for words!"

"That's interesting," said Lord Trumpington-Potts, thoughtfully. "I had no idea that there was so much money to be made in Grimely. You clearly have the ruthless money-making instinct which made the Trumpington-Potts fortune in the first place, back in the olden days."

"Really, Father? Please, tell me about it!" said Cecil.

"The first Lord Trumpington-Potts started off with nothing but a potato," said Lord

Trumpington-Potts, stroking his beard. "But before long, he was one of the richest men in England!"

"How did he do it, Father?" Cecil asked, impressed.

"Well, he told a very rich and very stupid man that it was a magic potato, and swapped it for a large bag of gold. He used the money to buy himself some fine clothes and then set up in business selling ladies' hats."

"And his business did well?"

"Oh, no," said Lord Trumpington-Potts. "He was terrible at selling hats. But it was a good way to meet rich ladies, and he was very good-looking, with a beard almost as magnificent as mine. Before long, he married a very ugly, but very rich noblewoman. The rest, my dear boy, is history! Now, let me see this form!"

Lord Trumpington-Potts reached for his

giant peacock-feather quill pen and
signed with a flourish. "Well done,
Cecil," he said. "You certainly
deserve to go on your school
trip. You may have ruined
several of my extremely
fine linen handkerchiefs,
but it was in the best
possible cause!"

Lord Frampington-Potts

Cecil was very proud to hand his bag of money and the form to Mr Coleman that morning.

"I am *so excited!*" he said, staring at Mr Coleman with wide and sparkling eyes. "This is going to be the BEST trip EVER!"

"I'm glad you think so, Cecil," said Mr Coleman. "Here is the equipment list – it's what you need to bring with you. We provide the tents, but you'll need a sleeping bag, a large rucksack, wellies and a good waterproof jacket. Have you got those things?"

"Well, I can wear Father's waterproof travelling overcoat," said Cecil, "and I have got wellington boots. But I don't have a sleeping bag or a large rucksack."

"Then you must buy or borrow these items," said Mr Coleman. "You must be properly equipped, or you can't come on the trip."

"Don't worry, Mr Coleman," said Cecil, marching back to his desk. "I'll be the best-equipped boy there!"

At morning break, Boogster went up to Cecil, looking embarrassed. "Want to come back to my dad's house after school for some dinner?" he said.

The gang had discussed the fact that Cecil had only beans and radishes to eat at home and had decided that even if he was the most annoying boy they had ever met, they should help him. In the next few weeks, each one of them would have him back for something to eat after school.

Boogster had volunteered to go first, because he wanted to get it over with.

"Go back to YOUR HOUSE? For DINNER? Would I? Of COURSE I would. You're the first person who's ever asked me back to their house, *ever*. I am SO HAPPY!"

Cecil was dancing around all through break time like a giddy goat, and for the rest of

BAAAAAAAA
BLEAAAAAAA

the day he told everybody he met that he was going back to Boogster's house:

"Have you finished your maths problems, Cecil?" asked Mr Coleman in class that afternoon.

"No, sir," said Cecil, beaming. "I am just BESIDE MYSELF! Do you know why? It's because I'm going back to Boogster's after school today!"

"No running in the corridor, Cecil," warned Mr Nutter at afternoon break.

"I can't help it, sir," said Cecil. "I'm running with happiness because I'm going back to Boogster's after school today!"

"Don't forget your book bag," called Mrs Magpie, the school secretary, as he ran out of school at the end of the day.

"It's because I'm distracted, Mrs Magpie," gasped Cecil, breathless with excitement. "I'm going to Boogster's, you see, after school."

Boogster was waiting for Cecil at the

school gates. "Is there anybody who *doesn't* know you're coming to mine for dinner?" he asked, sarcastically.

"No," said Cecil, "except Father, but we can call in and tell him on the way to yours."

The two boys called in at Cecil and Lord Trumpington-Potts's bedsit, and found Cecil's father looking doleful, washing his socks in the kitchen sink.

Boogster noticed how small and cramped the tiny bedsit was and that there was only one chair, and no television or computer.

"What's wrong, Father?" asked Cecil.

"Apparently," said Lord Trumpington-Potts with a rueful smile, "it is acceptable for a child to clean people's shoes at the railway station using spit and a handkerchief. However, when a grown man with a long beard tries the same thing, it is looked on as a *criminal activity*. The police were called, and I've spent the whole day explaining myself."

"Never mind, Father," said Cecil, "you'll find a job soon, I'm sure of it! Please meet my friend Boogster – I'm going to his dad's house for tea."

Boogster had seen Lord Trumpington-Potts before, but could not help staring at this strange, tall man with the longest beard he had ever seen.

"It's 9 Grimely Road," said Boogster. "If you'd like to come round later, my dad would love to meet a real lord."

"Certainly, young man," said Lord Trumpington-Potts, raising his top hat and bowing graciously. "It will be a pleasure."

Boogster's dad, Charlie, lived in a cosy terraced house. He was sitting on the sofa when they arrived, practising a song on his guitar. It was obvious that he was a musician; not just because of the guitar, but because of his cool sunglasses. He looked exactly like an ageing rock star.

"Pleased to meet you," he said to Cecil, shaking his hand.

"Hello," said Cecil, "I'm Cecil Trumpington-Potts, and your son is my bestest friend EVER. We're going on a camping expedition together, and I'm taking a hundred pairs of my panty wanty woos!"

"Cool," said Boogster's dad, going back to strumming his guitar.

"Can we play on the computer, Dad?" asked Boogster. "I want to play Death Battle Total Destruction Quest – it's great, Cecil!"

TWANG!

"Just for half an hour," said Charlie.

Cecil had started to learn about computers at school, and had got used to using the mouse and playing simple games. But nothing had prepared him for Death Battle Total Destruction Quest.

"I'm on Warrior Level 1,367!" said Boogster proudly. "Which means that I win most of my battles. Look, I'm just going to destroy this village. First, I'll kill the guards ... "

Boogster's warrior stepped forwards and chopped the heads off three guards, then entered the village followed by his battalion.

"STOP!" shouted Cecil suddenly, at the top of his voice. "HELP! POLICE! MURDER!"

Boogster's dad charged up the stairs and into Boogster's bedroom, still holding his guitar. In fact, he was waving it in the air as if he might have to use it to fight off some intruder. "What's happening?" he shouted.

"He's *murdering* people!" Cecil pointed at the computer. "And now the village is on fire!"

"Cecil," said Charlie patiently, lowering the guitar, "it's just a computer game. Nobody is actually dead."

"So what did they do?" asked Cecil, when Boogster's dad went back downstairs.

"Who?"

"The people in that village. What did they do to your warrior? Did they kill his family? Or were they plotting to destroy the world?"

"No," said Boogster, puzzled. "None of those things."

"So why did you kill them all?" Cecil was equally puzzled.

"To get up to Level 1,368 of course. I need to increase my power. Killing increases your power."

"Boogster," said Cecil.

"Yeah?"

"Can you teach me how to play football now?"

"All right," said Boogster.

Boogster had promised to teach Cecil the basics of football. The gang played at school, but Mucker had refused to let Cecil join in because Cecil had a tendency to skip after the ball swinging his arms in the air, which Mucker thought made them all look stupid.

"So the object is to get the ball in the goal," said Cecil, once they were in the back garden.

"How fascinating! Now, which foot should I use?"

"The one you find easiest," said Boogster.

"Both are easy," said Cecil.

"Just try and get the ball past me," said Boogster, waiting in the goal.

Cecil kicked the ball with his left foot and slammed it into the back of the net. Then he tried with his right foot and whacked the ball past Boogster with ease.

"Are you sure you've never played before?" asked Boogster, amazed.

"Never," said Cecil, "although I used to spend hours and hours kicking tennis balls around the grounds of Trumpington Manor, just for fun. I could hit every statue in the ornamental garden from thirty paces away, with either foot. I had to make my own entertainment, you see."

After they had had their dinner (Cecil had second helpings of everything), Lord Trumpington-Potts arrived, knocking on the front door with his silver-topped cane.

Boogster's dad, Charlie, looked at the lord's beard in amazement as they sat drinking mugs of tea and making polite conversation.

"So you are a musical family?" Lord Trumpington-Potts asked, looking at Charlie's guitar.

"Yeah," Charlie said. "I play in a band."

"I myself used to play the mandolin," said Lord Trumpington-Potts, looking wistful.

"Father, I didn't know you played the mandolin!" said Cecil, astonished.

"I have not played since your mother went

back to the circus," said Lord Trumpington-Potts sadly, "but perhaps I have left it long enough."

"Come round sometime and let me hear you," said Charlie. "Us musicians should stick together."

"Perhaps I shall," said Lord Trumpington-Potts quietly,  nodding to himself. "Perhaps I shall!"

The next week Cecil joined the school football team, at Boogster's suggestion.

It happened to be the monthly match between Grimely East Primary and Lofty Heights Primary, which Lofty Heights Primary always won thanks to being coached at great expense by a professional footballer, flown in from Brazil.

It was the beginning of the second half,

and the score was four nil to Lofty Heights. As usual, Mr Butter – the head teacher of Lofty Heights – and Mr Nutter stood by the sidelines, Mr Butter smiling smugly and Mr Nutter muttering angrily to himself.

Cecil was on the bench, his feet jiggling up and down with excitement.

"You're just the sub," Mucker warned him. "Don't expect to actually play."

But Cecil was ever hopeful.

The Lofty Heights team played a dirty game – hacking, shirt-pulling and diving at every opportunity. As usual the referee, who was a good friend of Mr Butter's, turned a blind eye to their antics.

"Foul!" shouted Bob angrily, as the worst Lofty Heights offender, a tall boy called Cuthbert, stamped on her foot for the third time. He just laughed, his friends joining in.

"Ref, that was a foul!" shouted Cheesy.

The referee chose not to hear him.

"Shut up, big ears!" hissed Cuthbert. "Or you're for it after school!" Cuthbert and his gang often picked on Cheesy when he was on his way home from school, because he had to pass Lofty Heights on his way. Once they'd stolen his rucksack and dumped it over a wall.

"I'm not afraid of you!" said Cheesy, defiantly.

"Oh, really?" said Cuthbert.

The next time Cheesy got the ball, Cuthbert and his gang jumped on him. They left him pale-faced, clutching his ankle where Cuthbert had kicked it.

"That was completely out of order!" Mr Nutter shouted. "Red card!"

The referee gave Cuthbert a yellow card as Cheesy limped from the pitch. His game was over.

"Cecil! You're on!" called Mucker. But Cecil was already on the pitch, running in enormous circles like a puppy out on its first walk.

He scored a goal within thirty seconds.

"How did that happen?" asked Mr Butter. "The boy's only just gone on!"

Cecil scored another goal two minutes later.

"He's so fast! He's going past them like a rocket!" said Bob, with grudging admiration.

"Off-side!" called the referee, disallowing the goal.

"What does that mean?" asked Cecil. Mucker took him aside and explained the rule to him.

"We have to work as a team," said Mucker. "You have to pass me the ball, and I'll pass it back."

"I can do that!" said Cecil.

Mucker and Cecil scored another two goals together, and Bob, boosted by the winning streak, scored a third.

Five minutes to go, and for the first time in years, Lofty Heights Primary and Grimely East Primary were level. Mr Butter did not look quite so smug. And Mr Nutter was not looking angry anymore.

"Get that skinny kid!" whispered Cuthbert to his friends.

The next time Cecil had the ball, they all closed in on him, circling like sharks. But Cecil kicked the ball so that it soared over their heads towards Mucker. Then he dodged and weaved past them easily. By the time Mucker passed back to him, he was in the perfect position to slam the winning goal into the corner of the net.

"We've won!" shouted Mr Nutter. "We've *actually won!*"

Cuthbert and his friends wouldn't shake hands after the match; they just brushed past the Abominators rudely.

Cuthbert glared at Cheesy and Cecil, his long, thin face twisted with anger. "We won't forget this," he said.

"That was well good, Cecil," said Mucker, in the changing rooms. "Only, next time, don't pretend to be a butterfly as your celebration. You looked like a right numpty. And why are you still wearing those diddling panty wanty woos?"

Mucker talked to Bob about it again, later on. "You've got to have a word with him," he told her. "Remember you promised?"

"All right," sighed Bob. "I will."

Bob's chance came quickly, because it was her turn to have Cecil back for tea that week. Cecil spent the whole day leading up to it jumping around with excitement.

"I like your house," he said, as they reached Bob's smart bungalow. The front of the house was covered with climbing roses, and there were pots of brightly  coloured geraniums on either side of the front door.

"Honking flowers," muttered Bob.

Bob's mother was waiting in the kitchen, wearing a flowery apron and arranging sugar-free homemade biscuits on a plate. Bob's younger sister, Sapphire, was at the kitchen table, drawing pictures of flowers carefully in crayon. She stared at Cecil with large, round blue eyes. She was wearing a giant pink ribbon in her golden ringlets.

"I have been *so* looking forward to meeting you," trilled Bob's mother, in what was obviously her best posh voice. "Should I call you Viscount Trumpington-Potts, or do you prefer Cecil?"

"Call him Cecil," said Bob, looking embarrassed.

"Delighted to meet you, Mrs Shepherd," said Cecil politely, giving a small bow. "Your daughter is my bestest friend, EVER. Well, equal bestest friend with Boogster. I went round to his house last week."

"Oh, *such good manners!*" said Bob's mother delightedly, clapping her hands. "So much nicer than Ruby's other friends. I do hope that you will be a good influence on my daughter. Especially with this camping trip coming up – I've been absolutely *dreading* what those terrible friends of her might persuade her to get up to. You don't get up to things, do you, Cecil?"

"Certainly not," said Cecil. "I'm a lovely boy. Well, that's what Nanny Drudgy always used to say."

"A nanny! How wonderful!" cooed Bob's mother.

"We're going out till dinner," said Bob abruptly, grabbing two biscuits from the plate on the kitchen table. "See you later."

Bob hustled Cecil out of the door and they wandered down the street, with Bob kicking stones in an angry sort of a way.

"Your mother seems very nice," said Cecil.

"Yes, she is; for an evil person," said Bob.

"Your mum's evil?" said Cecil, his eyes widening in surprise.

"Oh, yes," said Bob. "Don't be fooled by the nice hair-do and the homemade biscuits. She is actually plotting to take over the world."

"What's she going to do when she does?" asked Cecil.

"I'll tell you what she'll do," said Bob. "She'll

plant her lame flowers everywhere and make every girl and woman wear frilly dresses and ribbons in their hair. You can see how she's brainwashed Sapphire. Everybody will have to be nice and polite, all the time. It's my mission to stop her."

"Well, good luck," said Cecil. "Let me know if you need any help."

They continued walking for a while, then turned back for home.

"Now listen here," said Bob, as they neared the house, "I have to talk to you about your panty wanty woos. The gang says they have to go. They're an embarrassment to the Abominators."

"But I *can't* give up my panty wanty woos!" protested Cecil. "Nanny Drudgy sewed them herself. It was a labour of love. They have the Trumpington-Potts crest on them! It's a matter of duty that I wear them – and they're jolly comfortable, too."

"I've got to warn you," Bob persisted, "the gang's not happy about it. Not happy at all. I don't know how we can keep you as an associate member if you carry on wearing them. It's a fact. Just saying."

"Ruby! Cecil! Dinner!" trilled Bob's mum.

"You've got to think about it," warned Bob as they went in, "or else you could be in big trouble."

Cecil sighed. "But life would be so dull without them. I don't want to wear horrible, boring pants!"

Dinner was served on the Shepherd family's best china, and with their silver cutlery. It was lasagne with salad.

"This is *delicious*!" said Cecil, as he accepted his third helping. "For an evil mastermind who's plotting to take over the world, you're an excellent cook, Mrs Shepherd."

The next week, Cecil was asked to Mucker's house, where he was a great success because of his new footballing abilities.

"He's incredible!" said Mucker's oldest brother. "Cecil, you can come around here and play with us anytime!"

"I will!" said Cecil. 'Mucker is my bestest friend EVER, equal with Boogster and Bob."

Mucker showed Cecil his room, which he shared with two of his brothers. There was a single bed and a bunk bed, and hardly room for anything else. The floor was so covered in smelly socks, sweet wrappers and so much rubbish you couldn't see the carpet.

"When we go on the camping trip, I'll be fine," said Mucker. "A tent will be like a palace compared to this stinking room!" He paused. "I s'pose our house is rubbish to you, you being used to a mansion and a four poster bed and that."

"We don't have a mansion now," said Cecil. "We're in a tiny bedsit, which smells of cabbages. I prefer it, though, because when I wake up I can say 'Good morning' to Father without needing to walk for miles around the manor trying to find him, only to be told he's off on a camel-riding expedition. He even knows my name now. He always used to get it wrong and call me Cyril, or Percy, or Ralph."

"I'd like my own room," said Mucker, "so I could practise my magic tricks in peace."

"You do MAGIC?" asked Cecil.

"Shhhh! I shouldn't have told you – you'll blab it to everyone and they'll just laugh at me," said Mucker.

"I promise I won't tell a soul," said Cecil. "Please show me a trick, PLEASE!"

So Mucker showed Cecil a trick where he made a handkerchief disappear, and then he pulled twelve brightly coloured silk handkerchiefs, all tied together, out of Cecil's ear.

"I have a WIZARD for a friend!" shouted Cecil, looking at the multicoloured rope made out of handkerchiefs. "You have *special powers*!"

"It's only tricks," said Mucker, embarrassed, putting his magic equipment back in its box and hiding the box on top of the wardrobe. "I've got a lot to learn. One day I'd like to join the Magic Circle. Only the best magicians can join."

"You'll do it, Mucker," said Cecil solemnly. "I know you will."

"Remember," said Mucker, glaring at Cecil threateningly. "Not a word to anyone."

After tea, one of Mucker's brothers lent Cecil his bike and Cecil and Mucker rode down to the park to meet the rest of the gang, who were on their bikes, too.

"Don't you have a bike?" asked Cheesy.

"No, Father had to sell it," said Cecil sadly. "I loved my bike – I used to ride it all around Trumpington Manor. It was great for those long corridors."

"You rode it *indoors?*" asked Bob. 'That would be *brilliant!*"

"Yes, but riding outside with all of you is much more fun," said Cecil.

Finally, Cecil went back to Cheesy's house. Cheesy's mum took a lot of persuading to let Cecil come for tea at all, because she thought that all of Cheesy's friends were far too noisy. The Spencer family hated noise. So she was pleasantly surprised at how quiet and polite Cecil was.

"My name is Cecil Trumpington-Potts," Cecil said, kissing Mrs Spencer's hand and bowing. "Your son is my bestest friend EVER, equal with Boogster, Bob and Mucker. We're going on a camping expedition together."

"Oh, my!" said Mrs Spencer. "Please come in; delighted, I'm sure!"

Mr and Mrs Spencer and Cheesy's older sister Sally could not have been happier with Cecil. He quietly drank his juice and quietly ate his piece of cake, and then he had a quiet game of chess with Cheesy.

"At last!" said Mrs Spencer to Mr Spencer. "William has a friend we can approve of!"

Dinner was toad in the hole, and the Spencers were surprised to see Cecil have four helpings, followed by two helpings of trifle.

"I don't know where you put it!" joked Mr Spencer.

"Well," said Cecil, "it goes in my mouth, then I chew it up, mixing it with my saliva. It then slides down my throat and into my stomach, where it turns into a sort of disgusting sludge which works its way through my small and large intestines. Then the waste matter comes out of my—"

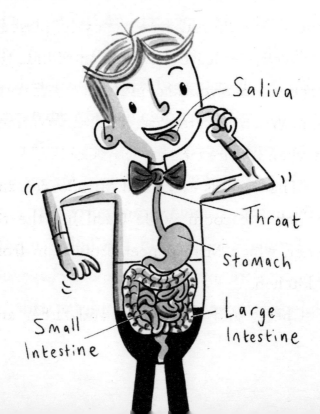

"I think we get the idea, Cecil," interrupted Mr Spencer hastily, as Mrs Spencer looked upset.

After dinner, Mr Spencer suggested that they all play a game.

"My father and I play a game called 'Hide the Tin Opener' all the time," said Cecil. "It's great fun."

"What a good idea, Cecil," said Mrs Spencer. "Would you show us how it's played?"

"Well, you leave the room and I hide the tin opener, then you all come back in and try to find it. When you are close to it I say 'Warmer' and when you are far away I say 'Colder'."

"That sounds easy," said Mr Spencer, and they left the room while Cecil hid the tin opener, which Mrs Spencer brought in from the kitchen.

Cheesy and his mother and father and

Sally came back in. They started to look around the room.

"Warmer," said Cecil. "No . . . colder. No, warmer! This is fun!"

Mrs Spencer moved over to near the fireplace, where the tin opener was hidden. Cecil got even more excited. "Warmer! Warmer! WARMER!!!!!!!" he shouted, jumping up and down and waving his arms. Mrs Spencer found the tin opener.

"You found it!" cried Cecil, "YOU FOUND IT!"

Mrs Spencer went quite pale, covering her ears. Sally looked frightened, and Mr Spencer shook his head.

"My family really, really, REALLY hate noise," Cheesy whispered to Cecil. "They're not used to shouting. In fact, it's banned in our house."

Cecil nodded.

"I shall be very quiet," he said, meaning it, "I promise."

"Perhaps a nice game of cards," suggested Mrs Spencer, taking the tin opener back to the kitchen, where it would cause no more noise and excitement.

They decided to play a game called "Knock-out Whist". Cecil proved to be very good at it. Soon it was down to Cecil and Mr Spencer with one card each. The trump was spades. Mr Spencer put down the king of spades. Cecil revealed he had the ace of spades. He completely forgot his promise to Cheesy.

"I WIN! I WIN! I WIN! I AM THE CHAMPION OF THE WORLD! OOPS! I'M MAKING A NOISE! SORRY!" shouted Cecil, jumping in the air and waving his arms around, then dancing in a circle.

"I think it might be time for you to walk Cecil home, William," said Mrs Spencer, her lips pursed in disapproval.

"Such a pity," she said to Sally after Cecil had gone. "He seemed like such a nice, *quiet* boy."

At last it was the morning of the long-awaited school camping trip. At ten o'clock on a Saturday morning, the children of Year 6 gathered outside the front of Grimely East Primary School, ready to board the waiting coach. The driver was loading their rucksacks under the supervision of Mr Coleman and Miss Jeffries.

All of the children were there except one.

Cecil Trumpington-Potts was missing. "Where is the noodle-head?" muttered Mucker.

"If he's not here soon, he's had it," agreed Cheesy.

As the last rucksack was loaded, Mr Coleman looked at his watch and announced that the children could board the coach.

"We can't wait any longer," he said, looking delighted. "The letter said ten o'clock, and it's now ten past."

"That's well dodgy. You'd almost think he *wanted* to leave Cecil behind," said Bob, suspiciously, as Mr Coleman hurried them aboard.

The driver was just starting the engine, and Mr Coleman was heaving a huge sigh of relief, when there was a cry from the back of the coach from the Abominators.

"It's Cecil! *Stop!*"

The driver stopped the engine. Cecil was standing by the bus wearing enormous wellies and an overcoat that was ten sizes too big. Balanced on his head was a small wooden trunk.

"What is the meaning of this?" said Mr Coleman, once the driver had opened the doors. "You were supposed to bring a rucksack!"

"I'm sorry, sir," said Cecil. "I don't have a large rucksack. But, as you can see, I am quite good at carrying my trunky-wunky on my head."

"Just get on the bus," said Mr Coleman.

Handing the trunk to the driver, Cecil jumped on the bus and went straight to the back to sit with the rest of the Abominators.

"What kept you?" asked Boogster.

"A domestic emergency," said Cecil. "My father got his beard trapped in the cutlery drawer. Somehow he had the end of it wound around the tin opener! It took me almost an hour to release him."

"Why didn't you just cut his beard off?" asked Bob.

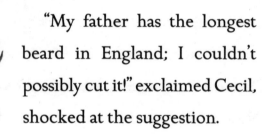

"My father has the longest beard in England; I couldn't possibly cut it!" exclaimed Cecil, shocked at the suggestion.

Up at the front of the bus, Mr Coleman sighed with disappointment – for a moment, he had hoped that Cecil wasn't coming.

He looked over at Miss Jeffries who was sitting in the seat

78

next to him and felt better immediately. He was going to enjoy three whole days in her company. Mr Coleman was sure that by the end of the trip, he would have the courage to ask her out.

Meanwhile, Cecil was getting a lesson from the Abominators on how to behave when you are travelling in the back of a bus: he was learning how to make disgusting faces at the people driving in the cars behind.

"That's right, Cecil!" encouraged Mucker. "Squash your nose flat and cross your eyes. Now hold this bit of paper up against the window."

Cecil held up the bit of paper, which, unknown to him, had written on it in huge letters: "YOU HAVE A FACE LIKE A BUM."

"The man in the car behind looks very cross," noted Cecil. "I think he is overtaking us so he can signal to the bus driver."

The bus pulled over and the driver got out and talked to the man who had been driving the car that had overtaken them. Then the driver brought the man onto the bus.

The man pointed at Cecil. "That's him! THAT's the boy!"

Cecil stood up. "I admit it, I was making rude faces. Sir, I am sorry if you found my squashed face insulting."

"You said I had a face like a bum," said the man. "*That's* what I found insulting. It's a disgrace."

"Sir," said Cecil, "I did not say you had a face like a bum, although now you mention it, there is a distinct resemblance."

"You held up a sign – it's in your hand!"

Cecil looked down at the piece of paper that he was still holding, and realised that he had been set up.

The Abominators looked at each other, wondering if he would let on.

"You've caught me red-handed!" Cecil said at last, holding up the piece of paper. "Name my punishment! I don't mind what it is as long as it's not being tickled with ostrich feathers. Or a lifetime in prison sharing a cell with murderers."

"He didn't grass us up!" whispered Cheesy to Boogster, impressed.

"Cecil, you can come to the front of the bus and sit in the seat behind myself and Miss Jeffries," said Mr Coleman. "We'll think of a suitable punishment for you later." He turned to the man. "I do apologise for my pupil's behaviour. He is, ah, not quite, um, *normal*."

"I can see that," said the man, getting off the bus. "Good luck with him; you'll need it!"

Cecil came to the front of the bus and

sat behind Mr Coleman and Miss Jeffries. "I promise I'll behave, Mr Coleman," he said. "This is going to be the best trip EVER!"

Mr Coleman relaxed back in his seat as the bus drove off again, and looked out at the passing scenery. It was a beautiful morning – almost as lovely as Miss Jeffries. He decided that he would remark to her about the scenery and was just about to do so when Cecil's head popped up between them. He was leaning through from the seat behind.

"Wonderful scenery," said Cecil to Miss Jeffries. "I've never seen so much of it before."

"How sweet that you noticed the scenery, Cecil," said Miss Jeffries enthusiastically. "I was just thinking how beautiful it was myself."

Mr Coleman frowned.

Ten minutes later, Mr Coleman decided that he would offer Miss Jeffries a toffee. He got the toffees out of his pocket and held them out. He was just about to speak when Cecil's smiling face appeared again between them.

"Thank you, Mr Coleman! My favourite!" said Cecil, taking a toffee from the bag. "I think you should offer one to Miss Jeffries, too; although I really don't think she needs one . . . after all, she's sweet enough already!"

Miss Jeffries giggled. "Oh, Cecil!" she said. "You *are* funny. Isn't he funny, Mr Coleman?"

"Hilarious," said Mr Coleman, bitterly.

By the time they had arrived at their destination, Cecil and Miss Jeffries were getting along tremendously. They got on so well, in fact, that Miss Jeffries had moved back to sit beside Cecil, leaving Mr Coleman to sit on his own. Mr Coleman had had to listen to Cecil telling Miss Jeffries tales of Trumpington Manor, to her obvious delight.

"I know that your father is a very intelligent man who is a leading authority on the history of the bucket, but I did not realise how well travelled he was," she said in an impressed voice. "And I had no idea that he was so accomplished at riding camels!"

They arrived at the campsite in time for lunch. There were lots of four-person tents already set up, so all they had to do was decide who was sleeping where.

"You're with us, Cecil," shouted Mucker, waving him over. "Cheers for not dobbing us in to Mr Coleman earlier. You did good."

"I'm sharing a tent with MY BEST FRIENDS!" cried Cecil, twirling around with joy. "It just gets better and better!" He bounded into the tent, where Cheesy and Boogster were unrolling their sleeping bags on their camp beds. Cecil opened his trunk and pulled out an enormous embroidered silk quilt, which he laid on his camp bed.

"What is *that*?" asked Boogster.

"I don't have a sleeping bag," said Cecil, "so I brought this. It used to belong to Queen Victoria, apparently."

"Cecil, you dingbat," laughed Cheesy, "we're supposed to be *roughing it*!"

"You're right!" said Cecil. "What was I thinking? It is us, pitted against the wilderness. Only the strongest will survive!" And with that, he rushed out of the tent.

"Where do you think he's off to?" said Mucker.

"Off to be strong and survive, I'd guess," said Boogster. "I give him five minutes!"

They all laughed. After all, the thought of Cecil surviving in the wilderness armed only with his panty wanty woos seemed completely ridiculous.

After unpacking, Mucker, Cheesy and Boogster went and found Bob, who was very annoyed with the girls she was sharing with.

"They keep shrieking!" she said, in disgust. "And they've all brought their cuddly toys with them. It's as bad as being at home with my mum and sister!"

They went and played football while Mr Coleman and Miss Jeffries unpacked sandwiches, drinks and cake for everybody and laid it all out on a camping table in the middle of the tents.

"Lunch, everyone!" trilled Miss Jeffries, in her lovely musical voice. Soon all the children were sitting in a circle, eating happily. Until Bob spoke up.

"Where's Cecil?" she said.

Mr Coleman searched the campsite, but there was no sign of him.

"He went to pit himself against the wilderness, miss," said Boogster.

"Ah!" said Miss Jeffries, smiling. "Well, if he is anything like his father, I'm sure that he will be an excellent explorer, and will be back safely soon. But really, he shouldn't have gone off on his own."

But after half an hour there was still no Cecil and, as time ticked on, Mr Coleman and Miss Jeffries were getting seriously worried.

"Do you think he's *dead*, miss?" asked Boogster.

Miss Jeffries burst into tears.

"We'll have to contact the local search and rescue team," said Mr Coleman, wondering if he could get away with putting his arm around Miss Jeffries. "And that means we won't be able to go on the hike we had planned for this afternoon."

"I can't believe you are thinking about our hike when a child is missing and probably in danger!" sobbed Miss Jeffries.

"Of course, my greatest concern is for the boy," said Mr Coleman, deciding this was not the right moment to try to put his arm around Miss Jeffries.

At that moment there was a cheer from the children. "It's Cecil!" they cried.

Cecil appeared before them wearing nothing but a very grubby vest and a pair of mud-soaked panty wanty woos. He was smeared

from head to toe in even more mud. His hair was filled with twigs and in one hand he was holding a lethal-looking bow and arrow, which he had obviously made himself. He was smiling from ear to ear, looking like the happiest savage in the world.

In his other hand he was triumphantly holding up a very big and very dead rat.

"I caught our dinner!" he said.

It was Mr Coleman who led the group into the mountains later that afternoon. He had been hoping that Cecil would be exhausted from his hunting, but after a quick shower Cecil was more than ready for adventure.

"This is the BEST fun I've had in my LIFE!" Cecil announced, appearing in his father's outsized overcoat, his face shining with pleasure. "Heigh-ho! Heigh-ho! A-hiking we will go!"

The other children were not looking quite so keen. As rain began to fall, most of them were wishing they were at home playing on their computers.

The hike seemed to go on for ever. Every time the children thought that they must be near the top of the mountain, they rounded a bend and saw a whole new stretch of path ahead.

"This is whopping hard work," puffed Mucker.

Cheesy, Boogster and Bob were also exhausted, having to stop every now and then to get their breath. Luckily, Mr Coleman was also finding it hard going in the drizzly rain, so he was not pushing them too fast.

There was only one person on the hike who was not at all out of breath. One person bounding forward with a spring in his step;

often running ahead and then racing back to join his friends. That person was, of course, Cecil Trumpington-Potts.

"Where does he get the energy?" asked Cheesy. "He's already been out hunting rats for two hours. How does he do all that on baked beans and radishes? It's unnatural, that's what it is."

Finally, they reached the top of the mountain. The rain had stopped and the sun came out. Suddenly, nobody was tired and grumpy any more; everybody was happy and pleased with themselves for having managed the climb.

"Look," said someone, "a rainbow!"

Spanning the valley before them was the most beautiful rainbow they had ever seen. They all stood in silence, enjoying the spectacular view.

It was a magical moment.

Until Cecil started to sing, loudly, and very out of tune: "Red and yellow and pink and green, orange and purple and blue . . . I can sing a RAINBOW, sing a RAINBOW, sing a RAINBOW toooooo—"

"Ssssh, Cecil," hissed Cheesy.

"What's wrong?" asked Cecil.

"It isn't cool to just sing like that," said Bob. "You're an embarrassment!"

"But I ALWAYS sing the Rainbow Song when I see a rainbow," explained Cecil. "Nanny Drudgy taught me."

"I give up," said Mucker, walking as far away from Cecil as he could.

Suddenly Cecil started to leap around in apparent delight. "Look! Look!" he cried. "OVER THERE! Down there, where we've come from, not far from the campsite – do you see? It's *Grimelyshire Safari Park!*"

"So what?" said Boogster. "It's a safari park. Big deal."

"It's not just ANY old safari park," said Cecil. "It's the safari park where Boris is!"

"Your pet bear?" remembered Bob.

"Yes," said Cecil, "and I'm going to take you to visit him – tonight!"

The Abominators discussed Cecil's plan most of the way back, and agreed that they would set off an hour after lights out.

When they got to camp, Cecil was very disappointed to find that Miss Jeffries had got rid of his giant rat, but was delighted to find that it was sausages and beans for dinner.

"I LOVE sausages!" he shouted, throwing

his arms up in the air. "I LOVE camping! I'm so happy I could burst!"

A little later, as the firelight from the big campsite fire flickered, and the moon shone above the mountain, everybody was sitting, quiet and content. It was a truly romantic scene: the perfect opportunity for Mr Coleman to ask Miss Jeffries to go out for a candle-lit dinner for two in the new fancy restaurant in town.

The moment would have been perfect, if Cecil had not been sitting between them.

"It's my birthday next week!" he announced. "I'm going to be a big boy of eleven!"

"That's wonderful," said Miss Jeffries. 'Do you know what you might get as a present?"

"He wants a bike cos his old man sold his other one," said Mucker, who was busy toasting a marshmallow.

"Oh, I'm not getting a bike, oh, no!" said Cecil. "We have hardly any money at all, you see. But Father says that he might be able to buy me a bag of broken biscuits, if he goes without baked beans while I'm away."

"A bag of *broken biscuits*? For your *birthday*? That's rubbish!" said Boogster. "You must be well gutted."

"I don't mind at all," said Cecil. "I've got

FRIENDS! I'm about to be ELEVEN! What more could I want? I don't need a present!"

"What an unselfish attitude!" said Miss Jeffries admiringly, much to Mr Coleman's annoyance.

At bedtime, the Abominators got into their sleeping bags fully dressed. It was time for Cecil's plan to be put into action.

The camp had been silent for a while when Bob appeared at the entrance of their tent with a torch. "Ready?" she said.

"Ready!" said Cecil. The boys grabbed their torches, and they all slipped out into the night.

Half an hour later, and after several falls after tripping over branches in the woods, the Abominators emerged at the entrance to Grimelyshire Safari Park. There were large gates, and the fence on either side of them was

very tall, with barbed wire along the top. There was also a hut near the gate, and they could see that a security guard was asleep inside.

"So, how do you expect us to get in?" asked Cheesy.

Cecil was studying the gate with narrowed eyes. "Easy," he said, and he produced a small piece of metal from his pocket. "I'll use my skeleton key – it opens any lock in the world. My father won it in a poker game from the Head of Police a long time ago. I've been carrying it about for years, but this is the first time I've needed it." He went up to the gate and used his skeleton key on the padlock, which opened immediately.

They crept past the security guard's hut and headed towards the bear enclosure.

When they got there, Cecil gave a low whistle. "It's my special signal to Boris," he explained.

Within a minute, the shape of a large bear emerged from the darkness. As the moon shone on him, the Abominators could see that Boris was a huge, handsome brown bear with deep-set, soft brown eyes. He looked gentle and intelligent. He bounded up to the inner fence around the enclosure and put his nose through, but Cecil was stuck behind the outer fence.

"It's good to see you, Boris," said Cecil. "Sorry I can't stroke your nose. I'd like you to meet my friends Mucker, Cheesy, Boogster and Bob."

Boris stared at each of them in turn and almost seemed to nod.

"Aren't you going to wrestle him?" suggested Mucker.

"Can't," said Cecil. "Boris might be tame,

but the others would tear me apart. Bears are very dangerous. But I can get Boris to do a few tricks for you. Boris! Stand on your head!"

Boris just stood there, and scratched his head sleepily.

"Boris!" said Cecil. "Do a cartwheel!"

Boris yawned.

"I don't think he's interested," said Mucker, looking at the others and grinning.

"Boris!" shouted Cecil. "Juggle!"

Boris yawned again.

"Yeah, Cecil," said Bob, sarcastically. "I'm sure he can juggle. Can he eat fire as well?"

"Boris," said Cecil, "we've come all this way to see you. Please do some of your tricks for my friends!"

Boris scratched his bottom thoughtfully, then turned sideways and did a perfect Moonwalk – he even seemed to wink at them

as he passed. After that he did a cartwheel, stood on his head and finally juggled with three stones.

"He's incredible!" breathed Cheesy. "You should have put him in the circus! You'd be rich!"

"I suggested it to Boris, when we had to

leave Trumpington Manor," said Cecil. "But I could tell he'd rather not. So you mustn't tell anyone what he can do. He's actually quite lazy, and he's much happier spending most of the day scratching himself and sleeping."

"Sounds like my dad," said Mucker.

After a while, Cecil said goodbye to Boris and they left the safari park the way they had come, with Cecil carefully locking the gate behind them.

"That was amazing!" Cheesy kept saying all the way back. "That was stonkingly brilliant!"

Little did they know that after they had left, Boris had decided that he would follow Cecil. As they made their way back to camp, the bear was determinedly digging under the enclosure fence.

The next morning, rain was falling heavily. Everybody was shivering as they ate their breakfast, despite being wrapped up in jumpers and waterproofs.

The Abominators were still full of excitement about the night before. Cecil made them swear not to tell anyone about Boris's tricks.

"Nobody would believe us anyway!" said Bob, as they ate their bacon rolls hungrily.

They were ravenous after their adventure. Cecil helped himself to three.

"I still don't get how you can cram so much food in your cake-hole," said Mucker, looking at Cecil in wonder. "Where do you put it?"

"He bounces it all off," said Cheesy. "Haven't you noticed he never sits still?" He was right: even at breakfast, Cecil was jumping around like a demented grasshopper.

Mr Coleman stood up. "This morning we are going on another hike!" he announced. There was a loud collective groan from the children. "We are going to hike up to that peak over there" – Mr Coleman pointed at a distant point – "and it could be slippery underfoot with this rain, so we'll all have to be very careful. People have died climbing on mountains, you know."

"Cool!" said Boogster, perking up.

They all set off an hour later, with Mr Coleman leading the way and Miss Jeffries following behind, making sure that everybody stayed on the path.

As the pupils scrambled up the rocky ridge, the rain seemed to grow heavier every minute.

Boogster decided to take advantage of the fact that Mr Coleman was out in front and Miss Jeffries was walking further behind. He made a very loud farting noise.

"Sorry," he said. "It was the beans last night!"

A minute later, Mucker followed suit, only his noise went on for longer. "Pardonnez-moi!" he said. "Those beans were lethal."

Soon after that, Cheesy made a farting noise, which lasted for over ten seconds. "Oops!" he said. "Better out than in!"

By this time, most of the class was laughing helplessly.

Mr Coleman stopped and turned around. "Enough!" he barked. "The joke is no longer funny. No more of those silly noises!"

They walked on for a minute, and then there was a loud, rip-roaring noise. It seemed to go on for ever.

"I'm really sorry, Mr Coleman," said Cecil. "That wasn't a joke."

Half an hour later, they reached a stretch of path with a steep slope falling from one side into a small ravine, which was about twenty feet deep with gravelly sides. Rainwater was gathering in the foot of it.

"Perhaps we should turn back," called Miss Jeffries, but Mr Coleman, who was some distance ahead, could not hear her.

Suddenly, a shape
loomed out of the rain
ahead of them on the
path: the enormous and
terrifying silhouette of a
giant bear, standing on its hind
legs and towering over them.

"It's a bear!"

screamed Mr Coleman,
in a not very manly way.
Everybody panicked. As one, they
turned and ran, sliding down the
steep sides of the ravine and gathering
in a frightened huddle at the bottom of it,
rainwater sloshing around their wellies.

The only person still standing on the path was Cecil.

"It's only Boris!" he shouted. "He's *tame*! He won't hurt you, I promise."

The children began to try to climb back up to the path; but while it had been easy to get down, it was impossible to get out again. Each time they tried to scramble up, they would slide back down again on the loose gravel.

They were trapped.

There was a sudden peal of thunder and the rain grew heavier. The water rose a tiny amount, so it was sloshing around their ankles.

"Help!" cried Mr Coleman, in a squeaky, scared voice. "We're all going to drown!"

"Nonsense!" said Miss Jeffries. "Cecil, I can't get reception on my mobile down here, but if you go back to camp you can use the emergency radio phone in Mr Coleman's tent, and call for help."

"Miss Jeffries, YOU CAN COUNT ON ME!" cried Cecil. "Boris! Take me back to camp!"

Boris obediently got onto all fours and Cecil leapt onto his back. The teachers and

other children watched in amazement as Boris and Cecil galloped off into the distance, back towards the camp.

"It's no use!" cried Mr Coleman, as rivulets of rainwater started snaking their way down the walls of the ravine. "We're doomed!"

"Stop panicking!" said Miss Jeffries. "Cecil will phone for help and the mountain rescue team will come and save us."

"He can't phone for help," said Mr Coleman.

"Why not?" asked Miss Jeffries.

"Because . . . I forgot to pack the emergency radio phone!" There was a long silence as everybody stared at Mr Coleman in disbelief. "And now the water's going to go over the top of our wellies! We're all going to GET OUR FEET WET!" he suddenly shouted, a wild look in his eye.

At which point Miss Jeffries slapped him across the face.

Mucker looked at Cheesy, who looked at Boogster, who looked at Bob, who looked at Mucker. The water was slightly higher. Mr Coleman was right. If it kept rising at this rate, it would soon be over the tops of their wellies.

"What's going to happen, then?" Boogster asked Mucker, who looked solemn.

For once, Mucker was out of ideas. "It's not looking good," he said.

As the minutes ticked by, they all got colder and wetter, and the water level got closer to the tops of their wellies. A few of the children who especially hated the idea of getting wet feet started to sob quietly.

Then they heard a call from the path

above. Cecil had returned, and waved to them from Boris's back.

"Never fear!" he cried. "Panty wanty woos TO THE RESCUE!"

He flung out his arm, and down into the ravine floated what looked like a multicoloured rope. Mucker waded over and grabbed one end of it.

"Pull yourself up!" called Cecil. "The other end is tied to Boris; he's rock solid."

Everyone watched, holding their breath, as Mucker tested the rope. The rope which was made of a hundred pairs of Cecil's panty wanty woos, tied together.

"It won't hold!" called Mr Coleman, who still seemed sure that they were all doomed.

But it did.

One by one, the pupils used the panty-wanty-woo rope to pull themselves to safety.

Miss Jeffries followed, and last of all, Mr Coleman scrambled back up to the path.

Miss Jeffries hugged Cecil. "Thank you! Thank you! You saved our socks!" she cried. "And possibly our lives! How did you think of making the rope?"

"Well, when I realised there was no phone, I knew it was all down to me," said Cecil. "I remembered a magic trick somebody

showed me with handkerchiefs and thought I
could do that with my panty wanty woos. It's
lucky I brought so many pairs with me, isn't
it?"

Mucker sighed. "I never thought I'd say
this, Cecil," he said, "but I don't know what
we'd have done if it wasn't for your panty
wanty woos!"

Cecil and Boris led everybody back to camp, with the children cheering all the way, glad to be alive even if they were wet and cold.

"Cecil saved the day!" they cried.

"No, I didn't!" said Cecil. 'My panty wanty woos did!"

Back at camp, Miss Jeffries made sure everybody got dried and changed, while Mr Coleman went to his tent to lie down.

"I don't think that Mr Coleman is very good in an emergency," commented Cecil to Miss Jeffries.

"No, I don't think he is either, Cecil," she said, "but some people are like that. They can't help it."

Which was just the sort of nice, understanding thing Miss Jeffries would say.

The rain stopped, and once they got a campfire going to help them all to warm up, everybody felt much better. Especially when Cecil gave them a magnificent wrestling demonstration with Boris.

"I'd better take him back to the safari park," Cecil said, after Boris had given all the children rides on his back around the campsite, "before they miss him."

"Then I'm coming with you," said Miss Jeffries. "Just to make sure."

The keepers, who were enjoying a cup of tea and had no idea that a bear had escaped, were very surprised to see Cecil and Miss Jeffries riding into the safari park on Boris.

"We owe you one, mate," said the head keeper. "Now our boss never needs to know. We should give you a reward or something."

"No need," said Cecil. "Just look after Boris and give him extra treats; that's reward enough for me."

A week later, back in Grimely, Cecil woke up filled with excitement, his eyes bright and shining. At last it was his birthday.

"It's my BIRTHDAY!" he cried, jumping up and down on the end of his father's bed. "I'm ELEVEN!"

As a special treat, Lord Trumpington-Potts gave Cecil a whole slice of toast for his breakfast, with butter on it.

"A whole slice of TOAST!" cried Cecil in delight. "With BUTTER! I'm the luckiest boy ALIVE!"

"I'm afraid that I wasn't able to get you that bag of broken biscuits, Cecil," said his father, sadly. "I was too hungry – I had to buy myself some beans or I would have starved."

"Never mind, Father," said Cecil.

Lord Trumpington-Potts produced a small package wrapped in old newspaper from beneath his beard. "But I did get you this," he said, his eyes twinkling.

Cecil jumped up and down with excitement. "It's a PRESENT, for ME!" he cried. He took the package and ripped it open. Inside was a twig, and on the twig was written in fancy squiggly writing: "Cecil Trumpington-Potts".

"My VERY OWN TWIG!" shouted Cecil. "It's just what I've always wanted. And you've put my name on it! So I know that it's mine! And you've got my name right and everything! Oh, thank you, Father, thank you! This is the best present EVER!"

Cecil did not walk into school on his birthday. Cecil did not run into school on his birthday. On his eleventh birthday, Cecil danced into school. That's right, he danced – as he had never danced before. There were jumps. There were twirls. There were pirouettes. There was even a knee slide.

"It's my birthday, it's my BIRTHDAY!" he sang, as he high-kicked his way into the classroom.

You might expect that the Abominators would be groaning with embarrassment at this moment. You might expect that Mucker would be saying: "Cecil, you lemon, give it a rest!"

But that's where you'd be wrong.

When Cecil danced into the classroom on his birthday, everybody cheered! And then they sang "Happy Birthday". Very loudly. Because Cecil was still a hero for saving everybody's socks and possibly lives on the camping trip, and when somebody saves your socks and possibly your life, you don't forget it a week later. You remember for at least a month.

Then something else good happened.

"You have some visitors, Cecil," said Mr Coleman, who was by now fully recovered from the mountain incident and hoping everybody would forget that he had been a giant panicking coward.

"Visitors! For ME!" shouted Cecil. "Is it because it's my birthday?"

The door of the classroom opened, and in walked the keepers from Grimelyshire Safari Park, wheeling a giant, shiny new bike. A bike that had at least fifty-one gears, including one for making a cup of tea.

"Happy Birthday, Cecil!" they said. "We heard from your friends that you could do with a new bike. After you saved our skins last week, we all clubbed together and got you this!"

Cecil did not at this point jump up and down like a frog, or a grasshopper, or a mad rabbit. He stood perfectly still.

Cecil did not at this point shout "HURRAY!" or "I'm THE HAPPIEST BOY IN THE WORLD!" or anything else. He did not say one word.

"Are you all right, Cecil?" asked Bob, touching his arm.

"Yes," Cecil whispered at last, in a very small, un-Cecil-like voice. "But can you tell me something. Is this real or am I still asleep?"

"It's real," said Cheesy, "and there's something else!"

"Something *else?*" Cecil's eyes were now like saucers.

"Yes," chipped in Boogster. "After school you're having a birthday party at my house, and my dad's band's playing!"

Cecil continued to stand in silence, taking it all in. Then, when he had taken it all in, he waved his hands in the air, did a special complicated dance involving lots of jumping and spinning in circles, and shouted, in his loudest voice ever: "THIS IS THE BEST DAY OF MY LIFE!"

And it was.

Boogster's dad, Charlie, had done Cecil proud, with a big table groaning with party

food. He had asked Lord Trumpington-Potts along too, who was looking very happy in the corner wearing a party hat and tucking into a plate piled high with every type of treat imaginable.

Everybody wore party hats and there were streamers and balloons. There was jelly and ice cream and cocktail sausages on sticks and apple slices and crisps and pizza and carrot sticks and ham sandwiches and little iced biscuits and grapes and cheese sandwiches and every type of cake and all sorts of other food.

Boogster did a demonstration of break-dancing to huge cheers. Bob did a headstand for over two minutes and got a round of applause.

Mucker, to everybody's amazement, produced an egg from Cecil's ear, and admitted that he did "a few magic tricks sometimes". And Cheesy shouted and made a lot more noise than he was ever allowed to make at home.

After lots of eating and party games and general fun, Charlie's band started to play. Everybody danced like berserk alligators and sang along.

"Come on, Lord T-P!" called out Charlie. "Give us a tune on your mandolin!"

"Oh, I couldn't possibly!" said Lord Trumpington-Potts, producing a mandolin case from beneath his beard.

"Go on!" everybody shouted.

And so he began to play along with the band, improvising with soaring scales and complicated harmonies.

"You're a musical genius!" shouted Charlie. "Why not join our band? We could do with another member."

The festivities continued until well past everybody's bedtime. And then a little later than that. Eventually, however, parents arrived to take tired children home, and everybody left, saying it was the best party they had ever been to in their whole lives.

Cecil and his father at last walked back to the bedsit, Cecil wheeling his brand-new bike and Lord Trumpington-Potts munching a sausage roll he'd found in his beard.

"Do you know the very best thing of all about my birthday?" said Cecil.

"What?" asked his father.

"This!" said Cecil, producing the twig from his pocket.

"I'm sorry it wasn't more, Cecil," said Lord Trumpington-Potts.

"Father," said Cecil, who was deadly serious. "I shall treasure it."

And so it was that Cecil Trumpington-Potts had the best birthday he had ever had in his entire life. And despite having a massive party and a bike with over fifty-one gears, his favourite present was . . . a twig.

Cecil Trumpington-Potts

About the Author and the Illustrator

J. L. Smith was raised in Scotland by West Highland terriers, but now lives in Buckinghamshire.

J. L. Smith enjoys cheese and brown sauce sandwiches, loves popping bubble wrap and always goes round revolving doors at least twice.

Swimming with dolphins, porpoises and whales is J. L. Smith's lifelong ambition but sadly the local swimming pool is not being co-operative.

Sam Hearn likes sandwiches too, especially cut into triangles and garnished with blueberries. His favourite activity for Tuesday afternoons is drawing pictures for J. L. Smith, of course.

Abominator Post

J. L. Smith would love to hear from you!

You can use the letter over the page,
or write your own

If you would like to include a drawing,
that would be even better!

J. L. Smith

c/o Little, Brown Book Group

100 Victoria Embankment

London, EC4Y 0DY

Dear J. L. Smith,

This is what I think about the Abominators:

_____

_____

_____

_____

My favourite character is:

_____

_____

_____

Best wishes,

_____